KLOOZ

The Night of the
Blue Heads

by J. Banscherus
translated by Daniel C. Baron
illustrated by Ralf Butschkow

Librarian Reviewer
Marci Peschke
Librarian, Dallas Independent School District
MA Education Reading Specialist, Stephen F. Austin State University
Learning Resources Endorsement, Texas Women's University

Reading Consultant
Sherry Klehr
Elementary/Middle School Educator,
Edina Public Schools, MN
MA in Education, University of Minnesota

STONE ARCH BOOKS
Minneapolis   San Diego

First published in the United States in 2008
by Stone Arch Books
151 Good Counsel Drive, P.O. Box 669
Mankato, Minnesota 56002
www.stonearchbooks.com

First published by Arena Books
Rottendorfer str. 16, D-97074
Würzburg, Germany

Library of Congress Cataloging-in-Publication Data
Banscherus, Jürgen.
[Nachts sind alle Glatzen blau. English.]
The Night of the Blue Heads / by J. Banscherus; translated by Daniel C.
Baron; illustrated by Ralf Butschkow.
p. cm. — (Klooz)
"Pathway Books."
Summary: When he is kidnapped, his head shaven, and painted blue,
Klooz is out to find who did it and why.
ISBN-13: 978-1-59889-874-3 (library binding)
ISBN-10: 1-59889-874-4 (library binding)
ISBN-13: 978-1-59889-910-8 (paperback)
ISBN-10: 1-59889-910-4 (paperback)
[1. Kidnapping—Fiction. 2. Mystery and detective stories.]
I. Baron, Daniel C. II. Butschkow, Ralf, ill. III. Title.
PZ7.B22927Ni 2008
[Fic]—dc22   2007006622

Art Director: Heather Kindseth
Graphic Designer: Kay Fraser

1 2 3 4 5 6 12 11 10 09 08 07

Printed in the United States of America

Table of contents

KLOOZ
The Night of the
Blue Heads

TOP SECRET

CHAPTER 1

A Call for Help

A few days ago I got my hair cut.

"You haven't been here for a while, Klooz," Mr. Cole said to me as he snipped close to my earlobe.

I like my ears. I was holding my breath until I was sure that he was going to leave them attached to my head.

I said, "The last time I was here was four months ago."

"Four months?" said Mr. Cole. He sounded surprised. "Your hair should be a lot longer than it is."

"I was busy with a case," I said. Then I told him all about my hair, or, I should say, about my not having hair.

The case began on a Monday evening. My homework was finished, and my mom had ordered a pizza for dinner.

Some cool music was playing on the radio. The crazy dog that lives above our apartment had finally stopped barking. It was going to be a nice evening.

I was finishing the last piece of pizza when the phone rang.

"You answer it," Mom said. "It's probably for you."

I picked up the phone and said hello.

A girl's voice asked, "Are you Klooz, the detective?"

"I am," I said.

"Come to 17 Oak Street right away!" the voice said.

"Why should I?" I asked.

"It's important. I am in—" Suddenly, the voice was cut off.

I heard a muffled scream.

I broke out in
a cold sweat.

"Hello!" I yelled
into the phone. "Hello!
What's wrong? Say
something!"

There was no sound
from the other end.

Then I heard someone
hang up.

Since I'm a detective,
I'm used to strange events.

Nothing really freaks
me out, but at that
moment, I felt like my
legs were made out of pudding.

"Who was it?" my mom asked.

If I told my mom what had just happened, she wouldn't believe me.

I wanted to find out what had happened to the girl first.

"It was Mike," I lied.

"Mike? From your class at school?" Mom asked.

I nodded. "Can I go over to his house?" I asked.

"Well, okay," Mom said. "Come home at eight thirty, Klooz. Not even one minute later!"

I stuck a pack of Carpenter's chewing gum in my pocket.

OAK STREET

I was ready, so I took off toward Oak Street.

To be honest, I felt really bad. I hadn't told my mom the truth.

Plus, I should have called the police right after that odd phone call. It might have been a case of kidnapping.

I promised myself that I would call the police right away if I found any evidence of a crime.

I got to the address the girl had given me: 17 Oak Street.

I was standing in front of a big, old, abandoned house. It didn't look like anyone lived there.

A few of the windows were covered with boards, and the front door was boarded up.

I didn't see any signs that something odd had happened here just ten minutes earlier.

There was a telephone booth in front of the house, but I didn't find clues there either. No clues anywhere.

I climbed onto a Dumpster, stuck a piece of Carpenter's gum in my mouth, and thought: What should I do?

Should I call the police? Without any proof of a crime, they would only laugh at me. Maybe someone was just playing a joke on me.

I decided to look around, more
carefully this time.

Right next to the front door there was
a window that had not been covered
with old boards.

I carefully pulled myself up to the open window and hopped up on the sill.

It was dark inside the house. Spider webs blew against my face.

I wished that I had brought my flashlight, but that couldn't stop me now. If you're afraid of the dark, you shouldn't become a detective.

I silently lowered myself to the floor.

Before I knew it, powerful hands pinned my arms behind my back. Then, a stinky sack was thrown over my head.

That's when I knew this wasn't just a joke.

It was another adventure for Klooz!

CHAPTER 2

The Blue Heads

I don't like playing Pin the Tail on the Donkey. Whenever people start playing it at a birthday party, I always slip away. I like to see what's happening with my own two eyes.

This was not a game. This was serious.

Then I realized that the phone call had been a fake.

There was no girl in trouble.

The open window should have warned
me that it was a trap.

With the bag over my head, I was
dragged through the entire city. Someone
was pulling me by the hand. I climbed
over a dozen walls. Sometimes I could tell
we were walking on a street or a sidewalk
or on grass.

It was impossible to figure out where we were going. Nobody could have done that, not even Sherlock Holmes.

During the entire time none of the people with me said a word. There were three of them. Two of them pulled me forward and the third pushed.

Think of something! I told myself. You are a detective!

"I have to use the bathroom!" I said.

We stopped. "Okay," I heard a teenage boy's voice say. "The little guy needs a break."

"You have to take this bag off of my head," I said. "I have to see where I am, you know."

"The bag stays where it is," another boy's voice said.

Too bad. My plan had been a pretty good one.

Even if I couldn't have seen who was dragging me around, at least maybe I could have been able to tell what part of the city we were in.

"I can't do it with a sack over my head!" I said.

"Then just forget about it," one of them said.

So we continued, over fences, walls, and broken sidewalks.

Finally we stopped.

I heard boys' and girls' voices and their quiet laughter, and then, finally, someone removed the sack from my head.

It was a relief to not have the smell of rotten potatoes in my nose. What I saw next almost knocked my socks off.

Masked figures stood around me in a room. There were candles burning on the floor and our bodies made flickering shadows on the walls.

Then, as my eyes got used to the dim light, I saw the craziest thing of all.

Every one of the masked figures was bald, and each one of their bald heads was blue!

I am amazed by how calm I was.

I should have been freaking out, but I felt like I was in a dream, and I would wake up at any moment.

"What's going on here?" I asked.

No answer.

"Why did you bring me here?" I asked.

Silence.

"Is this some kind of surprise party?" I asked.

No answer.

Then one of the masked figures stood and took a pair of scissors out of his jacket pocket. He pushed my baseball cap off my head. Then he started cutting my hair.

One clump of hair after another fell to the floor.

"Stop it!" I yelled. I tried to break free, but their hands held me in an iron grip.

"No!" I yelled. "Don't make me bald!"

It didn't help. The masked guy with the scissors whispered, "Hold still! It's going to be okay. We won't hurt you."

He kept cutting. Then he finished the job with electric clippers.

Finally he rubbed a stinky lotion on my bare head.

There was no doubt about it.

I was completely bald, but why?

Were they a special club for detectives, and this was my test to join the club?

Were they a group of kids from school playing pranks?

A cold wind blew on the bare skin of my head. I shivered.

"Why are you doing this?" I yelled. I looked down at the pile of hair that used to cover my head. "Why?"

No one answered. Someone put my baseball cap back on my head. Then they placed the sack over it again. Finally, they dragged me out of the room.

I knew where they were taking me.

After another tour of deserted streets, alleyways, walls, fields, and broken sidewalks, we ended up back where we started.

They pulled the sack from my head.

The big abandoned house at 17 Oak Street was in front of me.

I looked around. There was no trace of the people who grabbed me. They had disappeared as quick as lightning.

I took a deep breath, stuck a piece of Carpenter's gum in my mouth to calm my nerves, and took my cap off.

It was unbelievable. I didn't have a single hair on my head.

On my way home I avoided mirrors and windows. Klooz with a bald head? What did it all mean?

CHAPTER 3

Blues for Klooz

It was almost eight thirty when I got home.

My mom was sitting on the sofa reading the newspaper. "How was it?" she asked without looking up.

"Well . . ." I said.

Mom looked at me. "You sound funny," she said. "Did you get into a fight with Mike?"

"No," I said.

Suddenly she jumped up. "What happened to your head?" she cried.

She tore the cap from my head and stared.

Her eyes were getting bigger by the second.

"Does it look bad?" I asked.

My mom nodded.

"Why . . . you . . . no . . . hair?" was the only thing she got out.

"It was a trick," I answered.

I told her the whole story. All of it, down to the last detail.

"I don't believe all the crazy things that happen to you because of your detective work," she said.

"I know," I said weakly.

"So, you have no idea why they did this to you?" she asked.

"No, Mom."

"Have you seen what you look like?" she asked.

"No, Mom."

She took me by the hand and led me to the bathroom.

"Look in the mirror," she said.

I shook my head.

"Why couldn't they have just shaved your head? Why the color too?" she asked.

"Color?" I asked.

I was curious, so I looked in the mirror.

In front of me stood a small bald boy with a blue head!

Royal blue!

It was a nightmare!

That is what the stinky fluid the masked guys put on my head was for.

It was dye.

With one jerk, I pulled my sweater over my head.

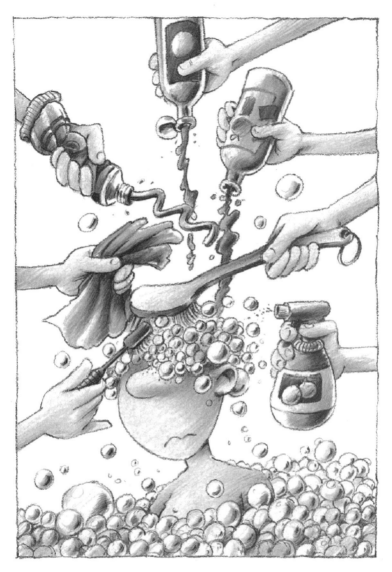

Before I knew it, I was sitting in the
bathtub with shampoo on my bald head.

I tried eleven different shampoos.

The color would not go away. In fact, after each shampoo the color got brighter. Finally, I just gave up.

"It's just not going to happen today," my mom said. "Let's go to sleep and we'll try again tomorrow."

That night, when I brushed my teeth I did not look into the mirror. I didn't like the guy with the blue head.

I opened the fridge, got out a bottle of milk, and poured myself a glass. Then I went to my room, stuck a piece of Carpenter's gum in my mouth and lay down.

I love Carpenter's gum. It almost made me forget my troubles.

My mom came into my room.

"Are you sleeping?" she whispered.

"No," I said. Now I'm going to get it, I thought. She's going to yell at me because I lied to her.

I thought she would forbid me from eating pizza for a whole month or something like that.

Instead she sat down on the bed next to me and patted me on the head. It felt funny.

"We'll get through this," she said. She gave me a kiss. "And you'll never lie to me again?"

"Never again, Mom," I promised.

* * *

The next morning, I was tired. I didn't want to go to school, but my mom said I had to. She tried to wash the blue off of my head three more times.

Finally, she said, "Just put a ski cap on. Pull it over your ears and no one will notice."

"I can't go to school looking like this!" I said.

My mom held my backpack in front of my face.

"You're going to school with or without the ski cap!" she said.

I looked out the window. The sun was shining brightly.

Mom is pretty cool. It's just that she takes school so seriously.

I grabbed my ski cap and left. Outside, it was sunny and warm. I felt silly for wearing a winter hat. Underneath it, I was sweating.

On my way to school I stopped to see my friend Olga. She runs a newsstand in town. I needed to see her because I needed more gum. Also, Olga often helped me on my difficult cases, and this was a really difficult case.

There was a line in front of Olga's that was as long as a gigantic snake. It took a while until it was my turn.

I told her what happened to me. I started with the mysterious phone call, and ended the story by telling her how I'd tried a million shampoos but none of them worked.

She listened with her mouth wide open in shock.

"Let me see your bald head," she said. "I'll give you two packs of gum."

Two packs? I couldn't say no. I looked around me to make sure no one else was looking. Then I lifted my ski cap.

"You've got to go to the police!" Olga cried with horror. "That's bodily harm, hair theft, and who knows what else!"

"The police?" I said. "What exactly would I tell them?"

We were silent for a while. Then Olga suddenly said, "They all had blue bald heads, Klooz?"

I nodded. "Just like me. Why?"

Olga leaned over the counter. "A few weeks ago there was something in the newspaper about bald people with blue heads. I can't remember what it was all about," she said. "Something about animals, too."

"Animals, huh?" I said. "Well, thanks for the tip."

"No need to thank me," she said. She pushed five packs of Carpenter's gum across the counter. "Those are free, Klooz. After last night, you need something to lift your spirits."

Olga is fantastic.

I put my gum in my pocket, and then I hit the road. I didn't want to show up late for school with a ski cap on. I didn't need the extra attention.

CHAPTER 4

The Dog Kennel

School turned out to be okay. I told the teachers and the kids in my class that my head hurt, and they left me alone.

My love of chewing gum and detective work are well known, so a ski cap doesn't make me seem any stranger.

Luckily no one tried to pull the ugly thing off of my head.

My blue head would have been the news of the week!

After school I just wanted to go home, have a snack, and start my investigation. I had Olga's tip: the blue baldies had been in the newspaper.

I thought that the people at the newspaper office could find the right edition for me. Then I would know how to start my investigation.

As I left the school building I noticed a glimpse of blue. It danced about a hundred yards from me, here and there, back and forth.

First I thought it was a balloon, but then it turned, and I saw it had eyes, nose, and a mouth. Yikes! It was one of the blue bald guys!

I decided to follow the person. This guy would lead me to the others.

I would finally know why they had stolen my hair.

Olga had said that the bald guys had something to do with animals. That's why I wasn't surprised when we headed toward the zoo.

As we got closer to the zoo entrance, the bald person turned down a side street. A few times, he (or maybe she) turned around.

Every time the person turned around, I ducked into a store entrance.

Was this person leading me into another trap?

No way! He couldn't have seen that I was following him. I am an expert at following suspects without them knowing that I am there.

At some point, the bald guy turned onto another street.

I followed him. There weren't as many people walking around.

I had never been in this part of the city. The yards were getting larger.

I heard a bunch of dogs barking somewhere nearby. The barking was coming from a huge dog kennel that had a big fence around it.

Suddenly, things happened lightning fast. As I walked by the rusty kennel gate, someone pulled the hat from my bald head.

Before I could turn around, two men came charging out of the kennel. They threw me to the ground. They were yelling the whole time.

One of them weighed at least a ton.

I wanted to scream, but all I could manage was a croak.

I was buried under the huge weight of a person.

"You troublemakers!" I heard the big man yell. "You criminals! You will pay for this!"

I had no idea what he was talking about. I wanted to ask the two men what I had done. They had decided to flatten me as thin as a postage stamp, and postage stamps can't talk.

Suddenly the big guy bellowed, "Look, Harry, the dogs!"

A second later I could breathe again. With amazing speed the two guys jumped up. They started chasing dozens of running dogs. The dogs had escaped through the gate!

Normally, I would have stayed and watched the fun. Instead I stood up, shook the dirt off, and ran.

I didn't want to end up squished like a postage stamp again.

I only stopped running when I got close to school.

I fell onto a bench and took a deep breath, waiting for my heartbeat to return to normal.

I could see stars in front of my eyes.

Then I noticed that people were looking at me funny. Some of the people were pointing, and others were laughing.

What was their problem?

Then I remembered: my ski cap was still lying on the ground near the dog kennel.

"Look at that guy," I heard a girl say. "He looks like an Easter egg wearing a T-shirt."

I tried to keep my head down as I snuck home. My anger at the bald guys grew every minute. An Easter egg wearing a T-shirt?

Wait until I found the guys who did
this to me!

As I walked through the streets,
my brain was working fast. What had
happened back there at the dog kennel?
Why were those two strangers so mad at
me? What did it all mean?

First I was nabbed, and then I was
robbed of my hair. Did somebody want
to get revenge for something?

Maybe it was a criminal I had
outsmarted in a past case.

On the other hand, what about all
those dogs? How was it possible for them
to all break out at the same time? Had
they been freed? Did the blue bald guys
free them?

I just didn't have enough information.
The only thing I knew for sure was
that I had been tricked twice. First
on Oak Street. The second time at the
dog kennel.

I had to find the blue bald guys.
Otherwise, I would never figure this out.

At home, I took a shower and put on
clean clothes.

Instead of the ski cap, I put on my
mom's winter hat.

Then I went in search of the blue heads, but there was no sign of them. Of course, they could disguise themselves by wearing different hats. However, I seemed to be the only person in the whole city who was wearing one. At least people had stopped pointing and laughing at me. After all, I am a private detective, not a comedian.

Suddenly, I realized I was out of gum. This was not a good day.

CHAPTER 5

Help from Olga

Olga burst into laughter when I walked back to her newspaper stand for more chewing gum. "Just look at you!" she gasped. She pointed at my mom's winter hat. "Are you dressed up as Santa Claus?"

"Ha ha," I growled. "Very funny. I need some Carpenter's gum. Three packs."

"Okay, Klooz," Olga said. "I have some information for you."

She shoved the packs over the counter and disappeared into her stand. Then she returned with a newspaper.

"I found this paper at home. Just look at that!" she said, pointing to an article.

The headline read: "Break-In at the Dog Kennel."

She handed me the newspaper and I started to read.

The article read, "Yesterday a group of young people broke into the dog kennel on Bright Street and released a number of dogs. According to the kennel's owner, the burglars were masked and had unusual blue, bald heads. The reason for the attack on the kennel is unknown. All of the dogs have been recovered."

"Does that help you at all?" Olga asked.

"It sure does!" I answered. "Now I know why they gave me a blue head!" I explained the whole thing to Olga.

"So the owners of the kennel must have thought you were part of the group who had freed the dogs," said Olga.

I nodded.

It was a brilliant plan.

The baldies nabbed me from the house on Oak Street that night in order to give me a blue bald head like theirs.

They tricked me into walking past the dog kennel and pulled off my ski cap at just the right time.

When the two men saw me, they thought I was part of the bald guys' group.

That gave the real bad guys time to free the dogs again.

These guys used me as a decoy!

"They have tricked you twice, Klooz," said Olga.

"I must be getting old and rusty," I told her. "It would never have happened to me before."

"You're still the greatest detective in my book, Klooz!" Olga said. "So, now what will you do?" she asked.

I shrugged. "I have no idea," I said. That was one hundred percent true.

I now knew why they had tricked me and why they had shaved my head. However, I didn't have a plan for finding them.

Olga was thinking hard. "You have to find the place they took you the night they grabbed you."

"I know I do, but how?" I asked.

Olga thought for a while. "What did it smell like there?" she asked after a few minutes.

"Smell? Hmm, like a cave." I replied. "Like something underground."

"There aren't any caves in the city," Olga said, "but the sewer is really smelly."

"It didn't stink like that," I said.

"How did the ground feel?" she asked.

"Dirty," I said. "Like a lot of dirt on top of cement."

Olga slammed her fist on the counter. "I've got it, Klooz!" she said. "The old warehouse! When I was a child, we used to go there to play."

The old warehouse! Why hadn't I thought of that?

"Boy, Olga, what would I do without you?" I said.

I started to walk to the old warehouse. My mind continued to work. There was still one question that I couldn't quite answer. Why had the blue bald guys let the dogs go? I hoped to get the answer soon.

The old warehouse looked like a
crashed spaceship next to a parking lot.

I found a small door that had been
boarded up. There was just enough space
for me to squeeze through.

A dark, empty hallway stretched away from me. The dusty floor was covered with footprints. I couldn't tell if the footprints were old or new.

I took out my flashlight and crept forward. The hallway seemed to be endless.

Suddenly I heard voices. I tiptoed further down the hall and the noises became louder. I saw a dim light coming from a door up ahead. I had to see what was beyond that door. Carefully, I peeked around the corner.

I didn't see bald guys with blue heads. No, there were just some regular teenagers sitting around. They looked like they were just a couple of years older than me.

They had plain old haircuts and plain old clothes. There were a few plain old candles burning on the ground. Next to them were four plain old dogs.

I quickly pulled my head back and thought to myself. This is where my head had been shaved, that was for sure. It smelled the same. The floor was the same. Why were these normal kids here and not the blue bald guys? What were the dogs doing here?

I peeked around the corner again.

The boys and girls were talking away. They seemed to feel at home here in the warehouse.

One of the boys bent forward. A ray of light from outside the warehouse lit up his forehead.

Aha! There was my clue! The boy had a bright red line on his forehead, the kind that you get when you wear a cap that is too tight.

The teenagers sitting in that room had all worn blue bald head caps when they had freed the dogs! That's how the blue baldies vanished so quickly after the raid on the kennel.

They just took off their bald caps!

I was the only person in the whole city with a really, truly blue bald head. They had changed my looks so that they could release the dogs and get away.

I stomped into the room. At first the chatting teenagers didn't notice me. That's why I ripped my mom's hat off my head and yelled, "Quiet!" I have no idea why I screamed, but it worked like a charm. In an instant it was so quiet you could hear a pin drop.

"What do you want?" a boy with glasses finally asked as he stood up.

"Are you the boss here?" I asked.

"There is no boss here," he replied.

I pointed to my bald head. "You did this to me!" I cried.

"No way," the boy said.

"And you let those dogs go!" I yelled.

"What are you talking about?" the boy asked.

I pointed at their red forehead stripes. "You wore caps during your raid. Blue, bald caps."

"You have too much imagination, kid," the boy said.

"I'm going to the police," I said. Normally I don't threaten to go to the police, but I had to this time.

My threat worked. A girl stood up. "Give it up, Scott," she said.

Her voice sounded familiar.

Was she the girl who had called me on the phone, and told me to go to Oak Street?

Then she asked me, "What do you want to know?"

"Why did you choose me?" I asked.

The girl laughed. "We needed someone who was curious and fearless. We had heard about you."

Ah, so that was it. I cleared my throat. "You were the one who called me, right?"

She nodded. "What else do you want to know?"

"Why did you free the dogs?" I asked.

"The owners of the kennel raise them to do tests on them," the girl answered.

"They find runaway dogs and sell them to big business," one of the boys said. He pointed to some dogs. "We were able to save these four dogs."

"But that won't change anything. The other dogs are still in the kennel," I said.

The girl frowned. "Something will change," she said firmly. "Now those owners know they are being watched."

"You should call the Humane Society," I said.

"We tried that," said Scott. "They didn't do anything about it. We even tried handing out flyers, but nothing helped, so we decided to free them."

"With me as your decoy," I growled.

The girl placed her hand on my shoulder.

"I'm sorry about your bald head, really. The first time we tried, the kennel owners almost caught us. Without you as our decoy, it would have been too risky for us."

I thought about it. "Why didn't you just ask me to help?" I said.

"You would have let us shave your head and dye it blue?" the boy asked.

I rubbed my head and grinned. "Well, probably not," I admitted.

"Are you going to go to the police?" the girl asked.

"No," I replied. "But if you think it is fun to run around with a blue head, you're wrong."

"It will wear off in a couple of days," the boy said.

"We picked that color because the Earth looks blue from outer space," the girl answered, "and we want to protect the Earth."

"But who protects my head?" I asked.

The boy held out his hand for me to shake. He smiled.

"It will never happen again. Deal?" he asked.

I shook his hand. "Deal," I said.

CHAPTER 6

Crazy Case

So that was the case of the night of the blue heads.

Wasn't it a crazy case? If all of my cases were as strange as that one I would give up being a detective forever.

If it hadn't been for Olga's help, I would have never solved the mystery.

The next day, I visited her newsstand. She handed me a letter and twenty packs of Carpenter's gum.

The letter read: "The chewing gum is for you, in order to make up for what we did to you. Signed, The Blue Baldies."

"They were nice young people," Olga said. "They came by this afternoon and bought the gum for you."

"Nice? Them?" I said. I rubbed my bald head. I could feel short hairs starting to grow.

The end

About the Author

Jürgen Banscherus is a worldwide phenomenon. There are almost a million Klooz books in print, and they have been translated into Spanish, Danish, Thai, Chinese, and eleven other languages. He has worked as a newspaper writer, a research scientist, and a teacher. His first book for children was published in 1985. He lives with his family in Germany.

About the Illustrator

Ralf Butschkow was born in Berlin. He works as a freelance graphic designer and illustrator, and has published more than 50 books for children. Critics have praised his work as "thoroughly enjoyable," "creatively original," and "highly recommended."

Glossary

curious (KYUR-ee-uhss)—eager to learn

decoy (DEE-koi)—someone who draws attention away, to lure into a trap

deserted (di-ZURT-id)—empty

evidence (EV-uh-denss)—proof that something happened

fluid (FLOO-id)—a flowing substance, like water

glimpse (GLIMPS)—to see something very briefly

imagination (i-maj-uh-NAY-shuhn)—the ability to form ideas of things that haven't happened

investigation (in-ves-tuh-GAY-shuhn)—a hunt for clues

kennel (KEN-uhl)—a shelter where dogs and cats are kept

nabbed (NABBD)—caught, taken, or grabbed

Discussion Questions

1. Why did the teenagers with bald, blue heads choose Klooz to be their decoy?

2. Klooz says that Olga is one of his best friends, and she often helps him with his cases. What are some of the ways Olga helps him in this book?

3. Can you explain why the teenagers had released the dogs? What do you think about performing experiments on animals?

Writing Prompts

1. The teenagers in this book care a lot about animals and about the earth. What are some things that you feel are very important? Make a list, and explain your answers.

2. Sometimes it can be interesting to think about a story from another person's point of view. Try writing Chapter 2 from the point of view of the teenagers. What do they talk about and think about as the chapter happens?

3. Imagine that your head is shaved and dyed blue. First, draw a picture of what you would look like. Next, imagine what your parents, teachers, and friends would think. Write a list of their responses!

Internet Sites

Do you want to know more about subjects
related to this book? Or are you interested
in learning about other topics? Then check
out FactHound, a fun, easy way to find
Internet sites.

Our investigative staff has already sniffed out
great sites for you!

Here's how to use FactHound:

1. Visit *www.facthound.com*

2. Select your grade level.

3. To learn more about subjects related to
   this book, type in the book's ISBN number:
   1598898744.

4. Click the **Fetch It** button.

FactHound will fetch the best Internet sites
for you!